FLUBBY

Flubby will Not Go to Sleep

To Mike—JEM

PENGUIN WORKSHOP
An imprint of Penguin Random House LLC, New York

First published simultaneously in paperback and hardcover in the United States of America by
Penguin Workshop, an imprint of Penguin Random House LLC, New York, 2021

Copyright © 2021 by Jennifer Morris

PENGUIN is a registered trademark and PENGUIN WORKSHOP is a trademark of
Penguin Books Ltd, and the W colophon is a registered trademark of Penguin Random House LLC.

Visit us online at penguinrandomhouse.com.

Library of Congress Cataloging-in-Publication Data is available.

Manufactured in China

ISBN 9780593382837 (pbk)   10 9 8 7 6 5 4 3 2 1

Flubby will Not Go to Sleep

by J. E. Morris

Penguin Workshop

I made a new bed for Flubby.

Flubby can sleep in his
new bed tonight.

Good night, Flubby.

Flubby will not go to sleep.

Maybe Flubby needs a
squishy pillow.

Good night, Flubby.

Flubby will not go to sleep.

Maybe Flubby needs a
warm blanket.

Good night, Flubby.

18

Flubby will not go to sleep.

Maybe Flubby needs a
sweet song.

Rock-a-bye,
Flubby, in the
treetop . . .

Good night, Flubby.

Flubby still will not go to sleep.

Why won't Flubby go to sleep?

Maybe he needs a bedtime snack.

I'll be right back.

Flubby did not need a
squishy pillow.

He did not need a
warm blanket.

He did not need a
sweet song.

He did not need a
bedtime snack.

Flubby just needed

a friend.

Good night, Flubby.